Monkey See, Monkey Do

A humorous
traditional story

This edition first published in 2010 by
Sea-to-Sea Publications
Distributed by Black Rabbit Books
P.O. Box 3263, Mankato, Minnesota 56002

Text © Anne Adeney 2006, 2010
Illustration © Christina Bretschneider 2006

Printed in USA

Library of Congress Cataloging-in-Publication Data

Adeney, Anne.
  Monkey see, monkey do / written by Anne Adeney ; illustrated by Christina
Bretschneider.
      p. cm. -- (Reading corner)
  Summary: The monkeys continue to outwit the peddler in this version of "Caps for
Sale."
  ISBN 978-1-59771-242-2 (hardcover)
  [1. Peddlers and peddling--Fiction. 2. Hats--Fiction. 3. Monkeys--Fiction.] I.
Bretschneider, Christina, ill. II. Slobodkina, Esphyr. Caps for sale. III. Title.
  PZ7.A261135Mo 2010
  [E]--dc22

                              2008050447

9 8 7 6 5 4 3 2

Published by arrangement with the Watts Publishing Group Ltd., London

Series Editor: Jackie Hamley
Series Advisors: Dr. Linda Gambrell, Dr. Barrie Wade, Dr. Hilary Minns
Series Designer: Peter Scoulding

Monkey See, Monkey Do

Written by
Anne Adeney

Illustrated by
Christina Bretschneider

SEA-TO-SEA
Mankato Collingwood London

Anne Adeney

"Chattering monkeys sound just like people talking. But what do they talk about? Perhaps this story will give you a clue!"

Christina Bretschneider

"I have two cats. They like to sleep on my desk or play with my pencils. I think they're just as naughty as monkeys."

"Grandpa Mojo," said Sunny.
"You look like you're wearing a
giant rainbow banana!"

Sunny's grandpa was a peddler
who sold colored caps.

"The easiest way to carry the caps
is on my head!" laughed Mojo.

"Now I must be off to the forest villages to sell them."

The villages were far away and Mojo
walked for hours before stopping
to sleep.

Mojo woke up and looked around.

"Where are my caps?" he cried.

"Give me back my caps!" he roared,
and shook his fist.

Each monkey chattered at Mojo
and shook its fist.

"Give me back my caps!" he roared, and stamped his feet.

Each monkey chattered at Mojo
and stamped its feet.

That gave Mojo a good idea.

"Monkey see, monkey do!"

he said to himself.

"Bad monkeys!" he roared, and
threw his own cap onto the ground.

Each monkey chattered at Mojo and threw its cap onto the ground. Mojo gathered up all the caps.

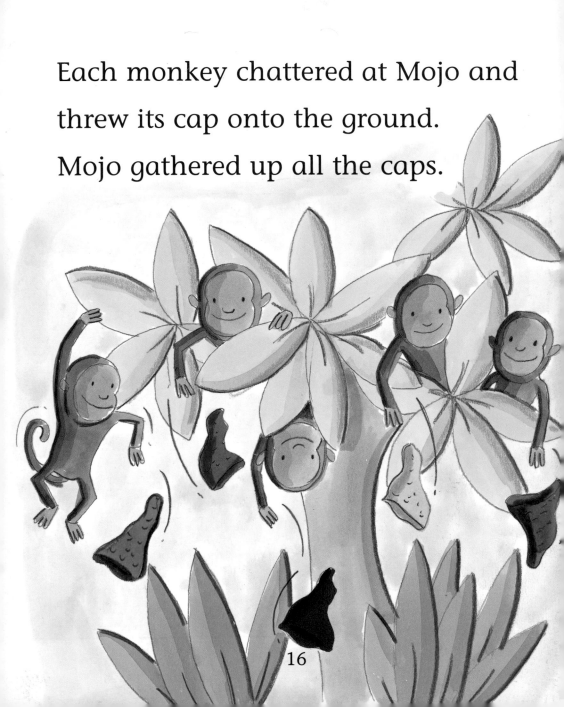

Then he put them back on his head and went on his way. "What a story I'll have to tell Sunny," he thought.

The years passed and old Mojo
stopped working.

Sunny was now a tall, young man.

He had always wanted to be a

peddler like his grandpa.

The villages were far away
and Sunny walked for hours
before stopping to sleep.

Sunny woke up and looked around.
"Where are my caps?" he said.

21

"Give me back my caps!" he roared, and shook his fist.

Each monkey chattered at Sunny
and shook its fist.

"Give me back my caps!" he roared and stamped his feet. Each monkey chattered at Sunny and stamped its feet.

Then Sunny remembered Grandpa
Mojo's story. "Monkey see, monkey
do!" he thought to himself.

"Bad monkeys!" he roared and threw his own cap onto the ground.

The monkeys chattered back at Sunny but they did not throw down their caps.

"Whatever happened to 'monkey
see, monkey do!' like my grandpa
told me?" wailed Sunny.

A monkey jumped down, picked
up Sunny's cap and put it on her
baby's head.

"You silly man!" said the monkey.
"Monkeys have grandpas too,
you know!"

Notes for parents and teachers

READING CORNER has been structured to provide maximum support for new readers. The stories may be used by adults for sharing with young children. Primarily, however, the stories are designed for newly independent readers, whether they are reading these books in bed at night, or in the reading corner at school or in the library.

Starting to read alone can be a daunting prospect. READING CORNER helps by providing visual support and repeating words and phrases, while making reading enjoyable. These books will develop confidence in the new reader, and encourage a love of reading that will last a lifetime.

If you are reading this book with a child, here are a few tips:

1. Make reading fun. Choose a time to read when you and the child are relaxed and have time to share the story.

2. Encourage children to reread the story, and to retell the story in their own words, using the illustrations to remind them what has happened.

3. Give praise. Remember that small mistakes need not always be corrected.

READING CORNER covers three grades of early reading ability, with three levels at each grade. Each level has a certain number of words per story, indicated by the number of bars on the spine of the book, to allow you to choose the right book for a young reader:

GRADE 1	GRADE 2	GRADE 3
50 words	130 words	250 words
70 words	160 words	350 words
100 words	200 words	450 words